GIFT FOR A GIFT

GIFT FOR A GIFT

ANNE ROCKWELL

Parents' Magazine Press / New York

Library of Congress Cataloging in Publication Data

Rockwell, Anne F
  Gift for a gift.
  SUMMARY: When the poor grasscutter uses his
life savings to buy a gift to honor beauty, he starts
a seemingly endless chain of gift-giving.
  I. Title.
PZ7.R5943Gi   [E]   73-12855
ISBN 0-8193-0711-4 ISBN 0-8193-0712-2 (lib. bdg.)

*For Hannah, Elizabeth
and Oliver*

In a shabby hut at the jungle's edge, an old grasscutter lived all alone. Each day he sold the grass he had cut, and then in the evening before he went to sleep he put almost all of the coins he had earned into a sack under his bed.

The years passed and the sack that held his coins grew full. One day the grasscutter decided to count his money and he found that there was indeed a great deal.

"How will I spend it?" he asked himself again and again, but he could think of nothing he wanted.

Then an idea came to him. He went to visit a friend in the village—a merchant who traveled from here to there, buying and selling. The grasscutter bought a gold bracelet set with a large emerald.

"Who is the most beautiful lady you know?" he asked.

The merchant answered without hesitation. "The Princess of Samarra!"

The grasscutter asked the merchant to deliver the bracelet to her with this message:

From someone who admires beauty.

And he gave the merchant a coin that was left, for his trouble.

So the merchant delivered the bracelet to the princess.

"How beautiful!" she said. "But tell me, who has sent me this lovely gift?"

Now ordinarily the merchant was a truthful man, but he was ashamed to admit that the gift came from such a poor and shabby old grasscutter. So he told a lie. He said that the bracelet was a gift from a fine nobleman.

"I must send him a gift!" cried the princess. "And I must send an even nicer one."

And so she did.

And she gave the merchant something for his trouble.

The merchant brought the high-stepping horse to the grass-cutter. But the old man had no idea what to do with such a splendid gift. What need had he for a horse?

"Who is the bravest man you know?" he asked the merchant at last.

"The Prince of Mamun. No Doubt!" replied the merchant without hesitation.

The grasscutter asked the merchant to take the horse to him with this message:

From one who admires courage.

The prince was as pleased with his gift as the princess had been with hers. Once again the merchant was ashamed to say it was from the old grasscutter. He told the prince the gift was from a princess who lived in a far country and had heard of his great bravery.

"I must send her a gift, too," said the prince, "for I am sure she must be very beautiful."

And so he did.

And he gave the merchant something for his trouble.

This time, without stopping at the grasscutter's hut, the merchant continued on his way to the palace of the princess. For what need did an old grasscutter have for camels and precious spices.

The old man was working in a field and watched with amazement as they passed.

And so the princess sent back a better gift, and gave the merchant something for his trouble.

The merchant's knees trembled with fear of robbers as he made his way to the palace of the prince.

When the prince saw what the merchant had brought him this time, he was worried.

How can I send a gift more splendid than *this?* he thought. But no one shall say that I am stingy!

And so he sent a bigger gift, and gave the merchant something for this trouble.

When the princess saw the barges laden with treasure drawing slowly through the water-lily pads, she was puzzled.

Her ladies-in-waiting giggled. "Surely the prince wants to marry you!" they said.

It must be so, thought the princess. I must meet this man!

The princess begged and begged the merchant to tell her where the prince lived, but he said, "Ahhhh...dear lady, that I cannot do!"

Nevertheless, the princess sent a bigger gift and gave the merchant something for his trouble. And she made a plan.

No sooner had the merchant left, leading the grand caravan, than the princess followed him. In each village she passed, she asked which way the caravan had gone. At one point, it was the grasscutter himself, working by the side of the road, who directed the princess. And so she traveled, always one day behind the merchant.

When the merchant arrived at the palace of the prince, the prince grew alarmed. For he was hard put to *match* this gift, let alone send a better one!

But he managed. It was everything he had, but he gave the merchant something for his trouble.

When the merchant was ready to leave, the prince drew his shining scimitar and demanded that the merchant take him to the princess.

"I must meet this lady who now owns all the riches of my kingdom!" he said.

Fearing for his life, the merchant agreed, and off they set for the palace of the princess.

They had been on the road less than a day when the prince saw a most beautiful lady approaching on a fine white horse. By the number of her attendants, he knew at once it must be a princess.

As soon as the princess saw the merchant leading the splendid parade of horses, camels, donkeys, and elephants, all laden with gifts, she knew they must be for her.

Quickly the trembling merchant presented the prince and princess to each other.

They instantly fell in love, and within the week the wedding was held. And they never did learn of the simple old man who was responsible for the whole thing.

Often, in the years that followed, when the grasscutter and his friend met, they would laugh together and wish the prince and princess happiness.

Anne Rockwell's first picture book, *Paul and Arthur Search for the Egg,* was cited as one of the Fifty Best Books of the Year by the American Institute of Graphic Arts. And since then she has written and illustrated many delightful books for children, including *Paul and Arthur and the Little Explorer, The Awful Mess, Gypsy Girl's Best Shoes, When the Drum Sang, The Monkey's Whiskers* and *Tuhurahura and the Whale,* all published by Parents' Magazine Press. Also for Parents', she has illustrated *A Gift for Tolum, Mexicali Soup, The Glass Valentine, The Three Visitors* and *Eric and the Little Canal Boat.*